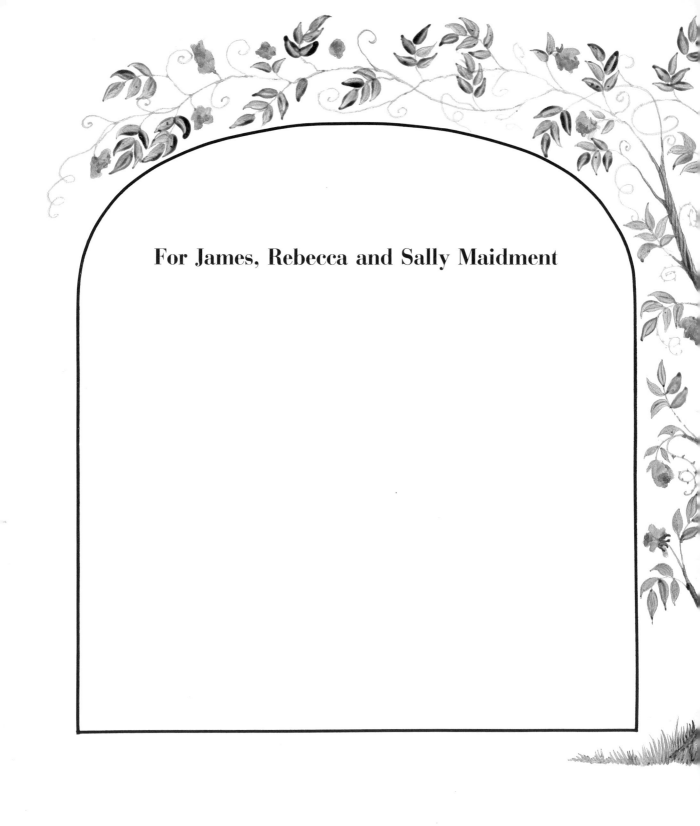

For James, Rebecca and Sally Maidment

Our Cat Flossie

Ruth Brown

Andersen Press London

British Library Cataloguing in Publication Data
Brown, Ruth
  Our cat Flossie.
  I. Title
  823'.914(J)   PZ7

ISBN 0-86264-120-9

First published in Great Britain in 1986 by Andersen Press Ltd., 20 Vauxhall Bridge Road,
London SW1V 2SA. Published in Australia by Random House Australia Pty. Ltd.,
20 Alfred Street, Milsons Point, Sydney NSW 2061. All rights reserved.
Colour separated by Photolitho AG Offsetreproduktionen, Gossau, Zürich, Switzerland.
Printed and bound in Italy by Grafiche AZ, Verona.

3   4   5   6   7   8   9

This is our cat Flossie.

She lives with us in London.

She likes the house and the garden, but does not
get on very well with the neighbours.

Her hobbies include birdwatching –

and fishing.

Flossie is a skilful climber

and an extremely enthusiastic gardener.

She always insists on helping with knitting

and making the beds.

She is very good at polishing shoes

but not quite so useful at Christmas-time.

**There are two things which she hates –
the sound of fireworks**

and visits to the vet.

Flossie loves collecting butterflies

and she is rather fond of snails

even though she finds them puzzling.

She is unable to resist a box

no matter what the size.

But, like all cats, most of all she loves to sleep . . .

and sleep . . .

and sleep.